Sick Girl Secrets

Anna Russell

An imprint of Enslow Publishing

WEST **44** BOOKS™

Please visit our website, www.west44books.com.
For a free color catalog of all our high-quality books,
call toll free 1-800-398-2504.

Cataloging-in-Publication Data

Names: Russell, Anna.
Title: Sick girl secrets / Anna Russell.
Description: New York : West 44, 2022.
Identifiers: ISBN 9781978595453 (pbk.) | ISBN 9781978595637
(library bound) | ISBN 9781978595477 (ebook)
Subjects: LCSH: Poetry, American--21st century. | English poetry. |
Young adult poetry, American. | Poetry, Modern--21st century.
Classification: LCC PS586.3 S535 2022 | DDC 811'.60809282--dc23

First Edition

Published in 2022 by
Enslow Publishing LLC
29 East 21st Street
New York, NY 10010

Editor: Caitie McAneney
Designer: Haley Harasymiw
Interior Layout: Rachel Rising

Photo Credits: pp. 1, 3-8, 12,13, 15, 16, 18-25, 27-31, 33, 40-44,
46-51, 57-60, 62, 63, 65, 67-70, 72-74, 77, 82, 85, 86, 88, 90, 95, 99,
105, 109, 112, 116, 118, 123, 126, 130-135, 140, 141, 143, 146-148,
151-155, 157-159, 164, 166, 170-173, 177, 181, 183 Infinity T29/
Shutterstock.com; pp. 9-11, 26, 34, 71, 75, 76, 78-81, 83, 84, 87, 91-
94, 96, 97, 100, 106, 108, 110, 111, 113-115, 121, 122, 132, 137-139,
142, 144, 145, 149, 150, 161-163, 165, 168, 169, 174-176, 178-180,
184-186 VectorSun/Shutterstock.com.

Printed in the United States of America

CPSIA compliance information: Batch #CS22W44: For further information contact
Enslow Publishing LLC, New York, New York at 1-800-398-2504

*To all the zebras out there waiting
to be heard.*

Life Under Glass

If you took a sample
of my life,
put it under glass,
peered at it with a
microscope:

things on the outside
wouldn't seem so different
from yours.

I'm this
        "normal"
girl.

I have a mom.
        A dad.

They're not together anymore,
        but it's not so bad.

Look   *a little*   *closer.*

I have a mom
        (who works
        day and night
        to pay for my
        surgeries, medicines,
        appointments,
        ...and more...).

I have a dad
        (who moved to Arizona
        after I got sick and
        I haven't seen him
        in two years).

        Look   *a little*   *closer.*

I have a caretaker,
        Mrs. C
        (because I can't take care
        of myself).

                Look closer.

I am this
        "normal"
girl
        (on the outside).

But inside,
        I am broken.

Closer.

Here's the secret of my life:

You have to
splice it open,

> dissect
> the cells.

Microscopic,
    miniscule,
        nanosized.

It's a little different
when you zoom in.

> (I don't want anybody
> to zoom in.)

Room for Waiting

Since I've been sick,

Mom and I do a lot of waiting

in rooms like the one we're in now:

> white walls,

>> plastic chairs,

>>> "music while you
>>> work" radio.

Since I've Been Sick

Mom and I do a lot of waiting

    for moments like these:

to find out exactly

    what's wrong

        with me.

This time,

Mom and I wait

        to see

if I'm ready

    (if this body is ready)

        to go back to school.

I'm not sure

    if I'm ready

        (if this body is ready).

Diagnosis (Noun):

The name given to

a pain,
a sickness,
a condition

that matches a patient's
symptoms.

Example of a diagnosis:

Ehlers-Danlos Syndrome,

a connective tissue disorder,
hypermobility of the joints.

Symptoms:

Chronic pain.
Bone dislocations.
Organ complications.

What This Means

My body is double-jointed.

The tissue that is supposed

to hold my bones together

is not strong enough.

Too loose,

like sticky gum

on warm concrete

that stretches too far

when you step on it.

My bones move,

and my muscles ache,

and my heart skips

some beats.

I was born with this body.

There is no cure.

This is my forever.

Muscle Memory

A nurse calls, "Natalie."
　　　My body rises,
　　　on autopilot.
　　　Muscle memory
　　　from all the nurses
　　　who have called my name.

Mom fiddles with my hair,

t w i s t s and s w i r l s.

"Mom," I say.

　　　"Sorry," she says.

Let's go.

Sometimes, Mom tells me
that she wishes she could

take all of my pain away.
She would do anything

to make it go away,
even if that meant

she had to take it
on herself. She tells me,

"Your pain will always
feel worse than my own."

If you've ever been sick,

      or if you know someone sick,

      you'll know that feeling

      of forgetting what to do with your

      hands as you wait.

"Want to do *Say, Say, Oh Playmate?*"

      Mom eyes my hands,

      the silver finger splints that

      keep each joint in place.

"Come on," I say,

      and I cup her palm

      in mine.

This is a game

    from Before.

Here's how it goes:

    Bounce your hands together.

    Clap once.

    Touch palms.

    Alternate.

    Clap again.

There's a rhythm to it.

    A comfort in knowing

    what will come next.

"He's Seen My Bones."

"That's a strange thing to say," Mom whispers.

We stopped our game when my wrist

let out a hollow

p o $p.$

"It's true," I say.
"He's seen more
of my body
than I have,
if you think about it."

"Most people go their whole lives
without seeing their own bones."

"I'm not
most people,"
I remind her.

Mom Sighs

Moves her hands

like she wants to

        hug me.

But I know she's afraid to hurt me.

Maybe she'll start the song again:

        Say, say, oh playmate.
        I cannot play with you.
        My dolly has the flu.

But I know she doesn't want to make me sad.

We're both thinking it, now:

How Madison and Abby,

        my closest friends,

stopped talking to me

        after I had to leave school.

What are they supposed to say

to the girl who is home

sick all the time?

Even Mom's friends stopped

coming over for dinner.

Is this what she told them?

Sorry, playmate.

I cannot play with you.

My daughter has the blues.

Taking care of her

is more important

than seeing you.

I almost ask Mom about them.

If it's because of me

that she works so much,

that she's lonelier than ever.

But Then

A knock on the door–

Dr. Atkins in his white coat.

I think

I can feel

my bones

t r e m b l e.

Fused

Dr. Atkins tells us
     that my shoulder surgery
     and the bolts in my ankles
     and the physical therapy
are working.

"This is great news," Mom says.
She takes my hand.
She hugs Dr. Atkins.

We are
     exclaiming,
     laughing,
     smiling.
But I am knotted
into a full galaxy
of nervous
energy.

Going Back

"So I go back?" I say.
"To school? To…
everything?"

"You've done wonderfully," Doc says.
"But you'll want to
take it easy."

"What do you mean?"

"Well," he says.
Trades a glance with Mom.

He pulls out folded
pieces of paper
from his back pocket.

I take them,
as though they are
brilliant, warm stars.

"This will help you
        manage the pain,
                and protect your joints,
                        and be independent."

Independence

Isn't that what
I want?

To go back?

To take care
of myself?

Unfold

The information on the sheets of paper
I hold in my palms

is for a

motorized wheelchair.

School Uniform

There's no
>official uniform
>for school.

But when I turned 13,
>and the pain started,
>I dressed myself up:

>>eye makeup
>>>(for the no-sleep
>>>dark circles)

>>short, styled hair
>>>(it hurts too much
>>>to wash and brush)

>>a perfect smile
>>>(to hide the truth–
>>>that everything hurts
>>>all the time).

I have to dress up to hide my secret.

>Because nobody at school knows
>I'm this sick.

Sick Days

All students take

        sick days.

The nurse calls home
    when you've got a

        sore throat,
        stomachache,
        migraine.

Since the surgeries,

    I've taken

        s e v e n t y – s i x

    sick days.

How do you go back

        after all   that?

Examined

The ride home
from Dr. Atkins's

is almost silent.

Just classical piano
over car radio.

Mom smiles at me. But
she knows something is wrong.

When we get home,
my caretaker is already there.

I move past Mrs. C,
to our downstairs bathroom.

Here, there's a perfectly round mirror.
I look closely at myself in it.

I know that I am standing here.
But I feel as though

I've been put under glass–
injected into a petri dish.

Is it the world that might examine me
through a microscope?

Or am I doing this to myself?

Metal Girl

I reach my fingertips
to the small spot
on my shoulder.

I lift my pant legs
and trace the outline
of the metal screws
in each ankle.

I think,

      maybe,

I am more metal than girl.

Star Glow

In bed, I see the stars.

I've had glow-in-the-dark

        ceiling stickers

since I was little.

      Way before we knew
      I would get sick
      and stay that way.

I made my own constellations.

      Created a universe just for me.

In this world,

      it's okay to feel

          aches,
          sharp pokes
          in my joints.

      It's okay that I'm not

               normal
      because

               normal

      doesn't exist.

A Body in Space

I think that's why
I like space:

we don't really know
what's out there.

Gravity-gone.

Foreign life.

Bodies don't work

the same way

outside this

stratosphere.

I thought, one day,

I could go to space.

Play with the stars.

Leave my mark

on the moon.

But they don't let
sick girls in space shuttles.

They don't let
broken bodies

soar that high.

Light Speed

After that appointment, everything moves

        at light speed.

Insurance approves
        the wheelchair.

The medical store
    fits it to my body.

They call Mom,
     and it's there.

Slick, black,
small wheels.

A joystick to move

forward,   sideways,

and back.

Wheelchair Girl

In the chair,
I take up
too much space.

I am too visible.
Like I have a bright
red arrow above
my head that says,

Look here! Look here!

Please don't look at me.
I don't want people
to see me like this:

muscle-less,
eyes-tired,
wheelchair-bound
girl.

Have You Seen This Girl?

If I made a poster

to look for the girl

I used to be,

it would look like this:

MISSING—

Natalie Brennan,

Five feet, two inches.

Brown eyes and brown hair.

The average 16-year-old.

She has d i s a p p e a r e d . . .

Gone. From. Her. Own. Body.

Have you seen her?

The Timeline of a Sick Girl

You might know me from

        Before:

        (When I could cartwheel
             or
        do the dishes
             or
        go to school.)

But now it's

        After:

        And every part of my body

                                  hurts
                                   all
                                   the
                                  time.

Time works differently

when you're sick.

Last Known Sighting

The girl I was before
was last seen

at the science museum downtown,
tucked behind the curtains

of the mummy exhibit.
This girl–

       13, three years younger
       than I am now–

breathes in the dust
of history in this room.

She sees wrappings
preserving bodies

from AD 300
and she leans in–

       without pain,
       without feeling each
       small bone
       shift–

toward the glass.

An ancient corpse
in centuries-old,
hardened cloth.

The girl looks closer.

She notices there's a small hole
near the teeth of the mummy.

Her breath fogs the clear coffin.
She sees its teeth,

small and crooked,
black like burnt popcorn.

The sight gives her the good kind
of chills. She spends

most of her time here,

remembering this—
how easy it was

to observe the past
without wanting it back.

Mr. Wilson, Principal: A Case Study

Mr. Wilson, my principal,
looks like:

shiny head,
pin-straight clothes,
soldier strut.

Sounds like:

deep voice,
rough, like he gargles
with pebbles.

Acts like:

he knows everything.

We have to meet with Mr. Wilson
Before I start school again–
this time with the wheelchair.

I tell Mom that I can walk
through the hallways
and to the meeting.

That I'm f i n e.

But I keep my head down
because I don't want
anyone to see me

before I'm ready
to be seen.

Mom, Mrs. C, and I huddle
into Mr. Wilson's office.

Mom gives him my doctor's note–
no gym for the rest of the year
because of my surgery.
He takes the note and grumbles.

Then Mom asks Mr. Wilson
what the school can do to help me
as I return after being gone
for so long.

Mr. Wilson's
crooked tooth pokes out
from his open mouth
as he explains

      504 plans,
      IEPs—

and that it will cost
the school a lot of money
to get what I need:

a lightweight laptop
to take notes
and tests.

(Because if I write
for too long,
my fingers,
and shoulders,
and everything
will hurt too much.)

There's no way
the school can get
me a laptop,
Mr. Wilson says.

It wouldn't be fair.
It would be too expensive.
The other students
would want them, too.

It makes me feel
kind of bad—

like it's my fault
I need to type
instead of handwrite.

If I could type,
my work would be

so much better.

And my body
would feel

        okay, fine, ready

for the next
assignment.

So...

Why is this—
using accommodations,
as they're called—

something so alien?

Something scary?

Something bad?

Mom and Mrs. C
start protesting,
loudly.

I sink into my chair.

But Mr. Wilson stops them,
says that if I want
to use a laptop,
we'll have to buy it
with our own money.

Mom pinches her lips
together in a tight line.

I know what she's thinking:
she's already working
overtime,

taking extra shifts
from the other secretaries
at the doctor's office
where she works

to file papers,
answer phones,
copy insurance cards.

My cheeks are warm,
red, and Mr. Wilson
says:

"We know you can do things
just like everybody else."

I think he means this in a nice way–
that he doesn't look at me
any different just because
my body works this way.

But I don't think I can
do things like everyone else.

Does that make me lazy?
A bad person?

Mr. Wilson tugs on his jacket
to make it perfectly straight,
and I say,

"It's not a big deal.
I can just write.
It's good for me
to use those muscles."

Mr. Wilson smiles, says,
"Good girl."

Mom pauses, looks
in my eyes for a long time,
before she agrees.

And I agree.

And Mrs. C stays
too quiet,

not wanting to say
what is on her mind.

So Mr. Wilson shakes our hands
and welcomes me back to school.

And that is that.

Out of Orbit

Mrs. C unloads the chair from the van
    (with me in it)

in the back of the school
    parking lot.

"Excited, girly?" she asks.
    I pause, then say, "I guess."

She unhooks the special belts
    that keep the wheelchair
        from rolling around
        in the backseat
        of her van.

"It's okay to be nervous," she says.
    "Mmhmm," I respond.

I don't realize
    my eyes are closed
        until Mrs. C
        places her hand
        gently
        over my surgery shoulder.

When I Open My Eyes

I notice that the sky is light

    and the outline of our moon

        nestles into the clouds.

When I was a kid,

    I used to think

        that the moon

            went away

    during the day

        to make room

            for the sun.

Now I know that

    the light from the sun

        is simply bright enough

            to hide it.

I Get an Idea, Then

"You know what, Mrs. C?

I think all I need
is a moment alone
before I go in.
If that's okay."

Mrs. C flashes a grin,
bright as moonglow.

"Of course," she says.

She leans down,
wraps her arms around me
the best she can
with the frame
of the chair
blocking my body.

"Go get 'em," she says.

"I will," I say.

*Normal Natalie
    is back.*

Day Moon

Once Mrs. C's van is out of the lot,

I jump to action.

Just like the moon,

my disability
doesn't really
vanish.

But just like the moon,

I can hide it away
by letting the sun
take over.

Around the Corner

just past the edge

of school,

there's an abandoned house.

My friends used to say

       it was the city's forest.
       With its uncut grass,
       the four-foot-tall weeds.

I wheel over to it,

       check once...twice...

I stand from the chair.

       (Catch my balance.
       Swallow down
       a burst of pain.)

I park it toward the back
       of the house.

I unclip the tote
        from my wheelchair.

Drape the strap
        across my torso.

        (See stars
        scatter my vision
        from the effort

        of lifting,

        of standing,

        of being
                normal.)

Now I Am the Sun

My secrets

are still there,

but I can be

bright enough

to hide them.

The Rumors Sound Like This

Natalie Brennan?

We haven't seen her

in months.

I heard she:

dropped out

broke her back

caught mono

transferred schools

died.

I don't think she's

coming back.

Do you?

I'm Fine

To teachers,

old friends,

the students

who stare:

I feel

like an award-winning

actress

all day.

But

I only have

one line:

"I'm fine!"

By Fifth Period

I have to get a pass
to go to the bathroom
and break down.

Luckily, I'm the only one there.

I am panting,
pressing my hand
to my side.

Each breath
shivers through my ribs,

sharp as scissors.

I turn my head,
stretch my neck,
hear each bone

pop.

The scar on surgery-shoulder
feels sickly cool,
like there's an ice cube
slowly melting,
dripping,
stinging the skin.

But I'm fine,

I'm fine,

I'm–

Not Alone

Just then,
I hear a flush.

I quickly straighten
my spine.

Pretend to breathe
without pain.

Fix a smile
to my face.

Riley MacDonald

exits the handicap stall.

She is the only student
who uses a wheelchair
in our entire school.
And she is so *visible*.

She always wears
bright, sparkly clothes.
Colorful jumpsuits
when it's warm enough.

Her eyes are the color
of honey and her soft brown skin
makes them look bright,

full of life.

"Hey." She nods at me.

I lower my gaze,
do a half-wave back.

"How's recovery going?" she asks.

A ping runs through me.

"Recovery?"

She turns to the sink,
scrubs her hands.

"I heard from Mrs. North
that you're back from
surgery."

      I silently fume at Mrs. North.

      I told everyone else
      that I was just sick, and that's all.

      Just sick. A bad flu, or cold–
      something normal.

      It's not the truth, of course.
      And my body is far from normal.

      "I–Yeah, but I'm fine," I say.

"Good," Riley says, unbelieving.

She lifts herself out of the chair
just slightly
to reach a paper towel.

      "Oh, do you need...?"

      What am I trying to say?

Do you need a hand?
A working pair of legs?

I don't know if I can offer
my physical help anymore.

"No sweat."

The corners of her mouth
tilt to an almost-smile.

Her left leg is shriveled,
her back twisted,

born with her muscles
underdeveloped.

You can see it on her,

her body's truth
shown on the inside
          and out.

"Listen," she says.
"I saw you in the parking lot this
morning.
In the wheelchair.

I know it can feel weird
in school with everyone
staring."

Suddenly, I'm looking everywhere
except her legs
and the wheels of her chair.

"But you're not alone,
you know."

I feel

seen.

And I want
to be invisible.

"Why would I feel alone?"
My voice is rough.

Riley's eyebrows squeeze together.

"There aren't a lot
of other disabled students
here, I mean."

"Well, I'm not. I'm not one," I say.
My skin feels too tight.
My shoulder burns.

Riley wheels herself to the garbage.
Gently places her used paper towel
into the bin.

"You can say the word.
Disabled."

She says it like all of her breath,
her whole heart,
is behind those three syllables.

"You can also use
person-first language.
Student with disabilities.
Some people prefer that.
I prefer disabled."

              "But I'm not...disabled,"
              I whisper.

"Okay," Riley says,
her mouth twisted
like she's bitten
into a lemon.

"I'll see you around, Nat."

Open Wound

Her eyes see through my muscles,
to the tissue
that won't hold my bones
together.

She knows.

She opens the door herself,
uses the wall to propel
her chair forward,
through the archway.
And then she's gone.

But on my skin,
I still feel that word
in her confident voice
like a tender bruise.

Learning to Survive

The remainder of the school week

d   r   a   g   s   b   y

so slowly,

so

painfully

slowly.

I survive my body's aches

minute   by   minute,

one
blink
at
a
time.

Each Morning

I stash
the wheelchair
in the bushes
of the abandoned house.

I start the day

sick

but I put on the greatest

show.

My Old Friends

Abby and Madison
are talking to me again.

I sit with them at lunch.

They want to go to the mall
and I pretend that's something
        I can still do.

Abby tries to get the scoop.
        "So you were, like,
        really sick, right?"

Madison asks,
        "How sick *were* you, exactly?"
        Scooches to the seat left of her,
        further from me.

        "I was pretty sick," I say.
        Let my hair fall over my face
        to hide my red cheeks.

"Ew. The SATs are coming up,"
Abby says. She crosses her pointer
fingers at me.
Stay away, her hands say.

"I really cannot get sick right now."

"Was it mono? COVID?" Madison asks.

> "It's kind of hard to explain.
> You can't catch what I had.
> Promise.
> I'm better now.
> Really," I say.

"If you say so," Abby says.

They ask about my schedule
to go to stores and start looking
for prom dresses.

I've convinced them

> for now

that I'm normal.

That everything is okay.

Choice

Out of the corner of my eye,
I see Riley MacDonald
look up from her book.

She has glitter
all over her cheeks.

She's not afraid
of people looking.

There was no Before
for Riley's body–

only a Now and Always.

We've known her as
the Wheelchair Girl
since kindergarten.

And, for a moment,
I hate her a little.
For not feeling ashamed.

For not having a choice
of whether or not to hide
      her disability.

Mrs. C in Orbit

At home,

               orbits
      C   around
Mrs.   me.

Fussing.

     Fluffing pillows.
     Fixing my posture.
     Filling the water pitcher.

She's been lingering in the mornings
when she drops me off at school.

I think she suspects something.

Mom must've told her I've been sleeping

         a lot.

Whenever
I'm not at school.

Whenever
I have 10 minutes
between appointments.

Whenever
I try to do homework–

Snooze City.

One Night

Mom asks me over dinner

about school,
my classes,
college options.

I pretend and pretend and pretend
that I can think of other things

besides

how much

my body

                  hurts.

Every small bone
in each of my fingers
burns like lit matches.

This happens after
I take notes by hand.

After I write out math
equations and scrawl
paragraphs in blue
test books.

But I don't want
to say how bad it is
because I don't want
to have to admit

that I can't do
what everybody else
in school

can do.

Sleeping Beauty

"I think I'm going to request
a meeting with Mr. Wilson," Mom says.
"See what kind of accommodations
you can get for classes and homework.
I'm worried they're overworking you."

> "I'm fine," I say.
> I've gotten good
> at saying this
> without even
> moving my mouth.
>
> "Honestly, Ma.
> I just had a lot
> to catch up on.
>
> Everyone's
> being really nice."

"Hm," she sighs.
"You look pale.
And the sleeping..."

> "I need my beauty rest,"
> I say. I stand from the table.
> Quiet the shaking in my
> legs. And kiss her forehead
> so she'll believe me.

The Pull of Gravity

Mom used to tell me
that parents always know
when their children are lying

because the air around us

feels
a
little
tighter.

I try to push Mom and Mrs. C away.
Put on a smile when they're around.

But they hover close,
as though they are fighting

the pull of gravity.

Pop

It's Friday,

the last day

of   the   long   week.

Finally.

Like every other day,

I start by making
my wheelchair vanish.

I have homeroom

     and English
     and math
     and choir.

My body starts talking to me
through
     pops
     cracks
     clunks.

Off

The ninth period bell releases me
from U.S. History

and my
        stomach
turns.

Something feels

                off,

as though the world
is tilted
        off
                its
                        axis.

"Shh," I say after a loud *snap*.
The ball of my shoulder
settling into the socket.

Riley sees me struggling at my locker.

She tilts her head,
asking me if I'm okay
with her eyes,
but I look
                        away.

My body doesn't feel stable.
I need to get to the abandoned house.

I need my wheelchair.

The hallways smell like
syrup, all sticky-sweet.

I tell my legs to move faster.

Out the doors.
          To the back parking lot.
                    Across the street.

My body is buzzing,
clicking and complaining
as each joint   *shifts*.

Something is
              off.

I go to the spot where
I've been keeping
the chair—

but it's gone.

Panic

I try not to panic
but

my muscles are
        fire-hot,
my knees are
        shaking.

I check around the entire house.

Nothing.

Spark

The wheelchair is gone.

Vanished for good.

I find my balance
by gripping a
rusty fence.

The fence chains snap.
Just as my

shoulder
        slips.

My ankles
        roll,
        twist.

And I fall to the ground

like a spark of heat

that's going to catch

        fire.

The Flames

In kindergarten,
the fire department showed us
the stop, drop, and roll.

How to crawl beneath smoke.
Test a doorknob first
before leaving a room.

They told us that the fire
spreads.
   Eats everything
     in its path
       in minutes.

In sixth grade,
we already had dozens
of fire drills.

We knew what to do
when the alarm sounded.

But the teachers looked around,
and we realized that it wasn't
actually a drill.

It turned out to be okay—
just a small kitchen fire
in the cafeteria.

But the worst part of that day
was that Riley MacDonald
was in class on the second floor.

You can't use an elevator
during a fire.

She couldn't leave the building
with the rest of us.

She had to wait in her classroom,

a l o n e

until a firefighter could carry her
and her wheelchair
to safety.

It's not the same,

I know.

But as I lay

in the weeds

of the abandoned house,

shaking,

broken,

I think I know how Riley must've felt:

waiting

to see if somebody would save you

or the flames would find you first.

Ashes

Mrs. C is the one to find me.

She'd driven around the neighborhood

in circles until she spotted me

on the ground

in a pile of weeds.

I tell her:

       please
           don't tell Mom,

       please
           don't call an ambulance.

But really, I'm thinking:

       please
           help me.

Mom meets us in the emergency room.

"Are you okay, Nat?" she asks.
She hugs me the best she can
around the sling
keeping my shoulder stable.

I mumble into her arms.

"I'm okay," I tell her.
I'm not okay, I think.

Her questions keep coming:

"What happened?
Why weren't you in your chair?
Why were you at that old house?
Why did you lie?"

Why?

My lips feel dry like ash,

the way they did
in first grade when I
excitedly volunteered
to try astronaut food.

Chalky and fake.

I can't really explain

why I did everything
        that I did.

All I can do
is whisper,

        "I just wanted to be

        normal."

When we get home
from the hospital,

Mom asks me to stay
in my room.

"It's not a punishment," she says.
It kind of feels like one.

It takes hours
for Mom
to reach the company
that customized my wheelchair.

It takes days
for Mom
to get them to agree
to send a replacement.

It will take months
for Mom to work enough
extra hours
to cover what insurance
won't cover.

And it might take forever
for Mom
to look at me
without shiny eyes
filled with fear–

waiting for the
other shoe

to

drop.

Smoke

Fire safety lesson number two:

even if the fire is out,
there could still be danger.

The smoke is the worst part.

It's the warning sign before the flames.

It's the reminder after the flames.

You have to wait for it all

      to clear.

I hear Mom and Mrs. C talking,

arguing.

Mom doesn't think
I can go back to school. Maybe ever.

Mrs. C tells her to give it time.
To let me heal.

I don't think she's just talking
about my shoulder.

Mom sighs real loud.

I can picture her pinching
the bridge of her nose
between her pointer finger
and thumb.

I limp back to my bed.

I can handle pain
when it's my own.

But I don't mean to hurt
the people I love.

I Think I See a Shooting Star

There—then gone,
just like that.

I hope that the star
can read my mind
because I'm not sure

what to wish for.

Two Weeks Later

Mom knocks
on my door.

It's been quiet
between us since
that day after school.

"Mind if I sit?" Mom asks.

      I make room for her on my bed.

"The new wheelchair arrived today."

      I nod, hold my breath.

"If you want to go to school," she says,
"then you have to use it."

      "I'm scared," I say.
      "What will everyone say?"

Mom pauses.

"Well, we can't control
what everyone else will say.
But you know what?

Here's what I would say:

That girl over there—

look how strong she is.
She listens to her body
even though it makes her
seem different."

"You think I'm strong?" I say.

Mom smiles.
She takes my hand.

"The strongest person I know."

"Okay," I say. "I'll try."

Meteor Shower

Once, before Dad moved
to Arizona, way west from here,

he took me on a walk
up a tall hill behind my school.

It was August.
I was small and not yet broken.

We sweated through
our tank tops, even though

it was night:
dark, starry.

When we finally reached
the tip-top of the grass hill,

Dad pointed to a place
in the sky. Said, "Look there."

I could barely see much more
than the normal twinkle of lights–

but then,   *there.*
A sudden shot of brightness,

a tiny smudge of outer space
entering our world.

Dad explained how meteors
worked: space dust and dirt

lit up by the sun's heat.

Zooming fast, fast, fast
into Earth's orbit.

He said,

"Sometimes it's easy to forget
how the whole galaxy
is so much bigger
than all our tiny, tiny worries."

I miss the things
he used to say to me.

Wheel Prints on the Moon

I return to school on the rainiest

day of the year.

I have to put plastic

over the new wheelchair,

its very own rain poncho.

People are going to see me–

      the sick version

      of me.

All my secrets.

      Suddenly visible.

Here's the truth:

A lot of people stare.
They whisper.

Even teachers.

Mr. Wilson sneers at me,
sour-faced.

I think about what he said
at our first meeting:

*You can do things
just like everyone else.*

I wonder if I'm letting him down.
Have I been letting myself down?

My face blushes hot,
but my body doesn't hurt.

And I think that's worth it all.

I think about things bigger than me:

this planet,
our solar system,
entire galaxies.

But here's another truth:

the stares, the whispers,
they don't last long.

Abby and Madison
wave shyly to me
from across the hall.

They don't ask me
if I'm sick,
or what kind of sick.

Because they can see now
that it's a different sick
than what most people have.

And by the end of the day,
this has already
become my

new normal.

I wait for the elevator
to go to my next class.
And as the doors open,

Riley MacDonald rolls out.

She has the biggest smile
across her face,

a sparkly yellow sundress
shining in the hallway light,

brighter than the sun.

"Nice ride," she says.

My lips tilt up, just a little.

Riley steers out of the elevator

and down the hall,

leaving damp wheel prints

behind her,

and I imagine

the moon.

Maybe someday,
right next to the footprints
on the rocky texture
of the moon,

there could be wheel marks.

superspoonie

That night, I get a DM
from Riley.

I didn't have your number, it says.
But I wanted to send you this.

Below the message is a link
to a vlog by someone named

superspoonie.

I shift to see the screen of my laptop,

and press play.

"Hey, spoonies!
Welcome to my channel!"

The girl on screen
has dark skin
and a scarf around her hair,
knotted at the front.

She has a full face of makeup:
glam eyelashes
red lips
glitter everywhere.

I want to pretend I don't notice
the tube taped to her cheek
that snakes into her left nostril–

but of course I do.

As I watch video after video,
I learn that she has issues
with her stomach.

Gastroparesis:
her intestines are
paralyzed.

She can't eat,
which is why she has the tube.

She calls it Jerome.

That's also why she has
something called a port
in her chest.

Every month, she goes to the hospital
and they use a needle to poke open
the small entry to the port.

This is where she gets things like:

>medicine
>fluids
>TPN

>(the nutrients
>we normally get
>from eating)

>right into her system.

Some of her videos are about this.
>Some are from her hospital room.
But there are others, too:

>her anniversary with her girlfriend
>big birthday bashes
>makeup tutorials.

I keep watching until I hear Mom
turn off the TV in the living room.

The clock says it's past one
in the morning.

I have to be up for school in five hours.

I start to close my laptop,
but then, before I can sleep,
I decide to do one more thing:

I open Riley's message and hit reply.

Thank you, I type.

*Maybe we can hang out
this weekend
and watch more of her videos.*

I press send before I lose my nerve.

Spoons

Riley and I make plans
to go to the mall
early Saturday morning.

I'm nervous,
      and excited.

      I want to ask Riley
      about superspoonie,
      about disability.

Riley's mom has room in her van
for both of our chairs
She drops us off
at the handicap entrance to the mall.

But Riley's mom calls it the
accessible entrance–
not handicap.

At first, I tell myself
that we use the accessible
entrance for Riley.

But then I remember:
these ramps
are for me, too.

We start by getting cinnamon pretzel bites.
They leave swirls on our fingertips
and sugar on our faces.

"So why is she called
superspoonie,
anyway?" I ask.

"Like the spoon theory," Riley says.
She pops another bite into her mouth.

"What's that?"

"People like us—sick and disabled—
use it to describe our energy levels.

Hang on," Riley says. She wheels
to the pretzel counter. She comes back
with a handful of plastic spoons.

"So let's say we all start with 10 spoons—
that's our energy—every day.

Most people might use
one point of energy, one spoon,

for exercising,
one for working,
one for cleaning...

That leaves them with
seven spoons. That's pretty good
energy, right?"

I nod.

"They can rest or go to sleep
and get some of those spoons
back. They might feel a little
tired, but the energy restores."

Riley gathers the spoons
into her grasp
like they're a bouquet of flowers.

"Now.
For

people
like
us..."

She meets my eyes with hers.
I think back to our conversation
in the bathroom at school.

How I said that I was
definitely,
100
percent,

not
like
her.

My cheeks feel warm.

Riley continues.

"Getting out of bed takes a spoon."
        She places one on the table.

"Showering takes another—maybe two."
        Two more go down.

"A whole school day?
That's, like, a billion spoons
but we'll say it takes five."

She's only holding two now.

"Homework."

One.

"Anything extra, well..."

Her hands are empty.

I look at the spoons
on the table. My heart beats loud.
I think of all the time
I spend sleeping.

Trying to fight
the need to rest.

Riley keeps going:

"One night of sleep,
if it's good,
might bring back
half the spoons
you started with.

You see,
they go so fast
for us
and don't come back
so easy."

Riley collects the spoons again,
tucks them into a bag
on the side of her chair.

"We're spoonies,
just trying to save our energy.
Just trying to make it through."

Make Some Space

This becomes our thing:

going to the mall every weekend,
eating pretzels,
watching new superspoonie videos.

At first, I avoid going in stores
that look small.

  "I'll stay out here," I'd say to Riley.

Everything felt a little too crowded.
The handles of my chair would catch on clothes.
My wheels would screech on metal racks.

But Riley said that we're not the problem.

"We're human. We want to shop," she said.

"Sure, we get around differently,
but they should think about that
when designing these stores."

One weekend, she tells me to
face my fears.

"Are you sure about this?" I ask.

She gives a wicked grin.
"Positive," she says.

I go in first, and she follows behind.

It's a crystal store.
Ceiling to floor–
sparkling and breakable.

"Uh," the store clerk says.

"Oh, we're just browsing," Riley says.

We do a few laps around the small store,
the clerk sweating behind the counter,
watching our every turn.

Riley tries on a necklace.

I ask to see a porcelain figurine.

After we see everything there,
after our wheels cover every inch
of that store,

we thank the clerk
and roll out.

We barely make it
around the corner
before bursting
into laughter.

People nearby look at us:

two disabled girls
laughing.

They're probably thinking:

"What could they be so happy about?"

That only makes us
laugh louder.

An Enchanted Night

At school that week
the flyers go up
for Junior Prom.

When I think prom,
        I picture:

        strobe lights

        pumping music

        dates and dancing.

There are two of those things
that I don't think I can do.

        (Hint:
        I've never been on a date.
        And I don't think my body
        is quite up to dancing.)

I don't think that Riley
will be into prom either.
But she wheels
to my locker
with a flyer.

I learn that when Riley thinks of prom,
she pictures:

fruity punch

laughter

her online friends

maybe
just a little trouble.

The theme this year
is *enchanted night*:

               magic

               mystery

               music.

"We definitely have to go,"
     Riley says.

And just like that–

                some sort of magic–

I'm in.

Prom Squad

Mom
& Mrs. MacDonald
& Riley
& me.

We call ourselves
the
Prom Squad.

Riley and I roll
around Macy's,
touching

lace
& silk
& tulle.

Our moms help us
in the fitting rooms.

Riley wheels out in

poofy pink
& seafoam green
& frilly lace.

None of it is right for her.

I step out in

shiny purple
& baby blue beads
& a yellow minidress.

I wouldn't usually want
to show my legs
with the weak muscles
and ankle scars.

But with the Prom Squad,
it's all okay.

I give a slow twirl,
and Mom snaps pics,
and then:

Riley reverses
from the changing room
in the most Riley Outfit

I've ever seen:

a black glittery jumpsuit
with a big bow
around the waist.

"Wow," Mom says.

She's right:

W O W

Just when I think
I'll never find a dress
that is *me*,

I see a flowy dress
the color of the night sky
with stars blinking
from the bottom
all the way up.

My own galaxy.

For the first time,
I'm actually excited
for people to see me.

To notice me.

The girl in the wheelchair,
more than her scars
and wimpy legs.

It's been a while
since I've wanted to be
visible.

Not Here

Everything feels good
for a while.

Until Riley and I pass each other
in the hallway later that week.

Bump wheels in our own
type of hug.

And she tells me that she can't
hang out next weekend.

"We have to talk," she says.
She turns her head,

her chair going with her.
"Somewhere...not here."

We plan to meet during sixth period
in the bathroom where we first talked

—before we were friends.
So much has changed since then.

I ask my math teacher, Ms. Johnson,
for a bathroom pass and she waves

for me to just go. Five minutes.
That's all I'll have to talk to Riley,

and I hope it's enough.
Riley is already in the bathroom

when I arrive. She's pacing,
forward and back, like a rocking chair.

     "What's going on?" I ask.

"It's Mr. Wilson," she says.

The Gym Rule

She explains:

Mr. Wilson is the head of everything—
    and people do what he says.

Riley found out that she's behind
    on class credits—specifically,
    one class's credits:
    gym.

Riley does physical therapy
    instead of gym:

        gentle stretches,
        slow movements,
        controlled exercises.

        This is what her body needs.

        This is what *our* bodies need.

Mr. Wilson won't make an
    exception for Riley for the
    gym credit that all juniors need
    to pass to the next grade.

The only option:
    Riley has to write 10 essays
    on the 10 sports units
    they cover in gym.

If she doesn't write the papers–
on an impossible deadline–
then Mr. Wilson won't let
her pass 11th grade.

       "How is that even allowed?" I ask.
       "You do physical therapy."

"I don't know."

Riley's mouth is moving so fast.
We only have a few minutes

before we need to go back to class
and act like this isn't happening.

       "I guess you have a lot
       of essay-writing to do," I say.

Riley rolls her eyes.
"No way. I'm not
going to waste my time
writing about sports
when I have Shakespeare
to read and SATs to study for."

       "Well...what are you going to do?"

"Nat, this is worse than you know.
My parents want to sue the district."

       "Like, for money?"

"Not really. Just to say
that this isn't right–

that you can't make
disabled students

do busywork just because
they can't do what other students
can do," she says.

I try to process quickly.

I picture lawyers,
a courtroom,
people screaming,

"Objection!"

But I don't think
this is what Riley means.

> "But wait," I say.
> "How does that change our
> plans for next
> weekend?"

Riley pauses.
Looks down.

"We're touring
St. Jude's Academy," she says.

St. Jude's Academy is the school
for only the smartest
science students.

And it's an hour and a half
from here.

I put it together, then:

Riley might have to move.

Listen

Mom is working a lot this week.

        Mrs. C has to help me

with everything.

She makes mac and cheese

        on the stove.

I watch from the dining table.

She rubs the flesh along her spine,

        and I remember

that sometimes she has pain, too.

She says it's her old bones.

        Maybe true.

I wish I could help.

I want to reach out,

        grab the pot, take the weight

of me off of her shoulders.

But we both know

it would be dangerous for me

to lift something heavy,

or stand for too long.

So instead, I tell Mrs. C

about Riley and Mr. Wilson.

She stays quiet

for a long time when I'm done.

She doesn't talk much,

but when she does,

it's important.

"Listen," Mrs. C says,

"Mr. Wilson

is the kind of person

who only cares

about his own wallet.

Your body is just

another cost to him.

But he doesn't live

with pain like you do.

All he knows

is the coldness

that chills his

body frozen.

I don't think

that man can

feel anything at all."

This

Before bed that night,

as I'm scrolling through

images on PicPost,

I see that Riley

shared the newest superspoonie video.

The caption only says, "This."

I press play and superspoonie

doesn't have her normal

supersmile across her face.

"Hey, spoonies, and welcome

to another video," she says.

"I want to talk about something

kind of serious—kind of sad."

She pauses and the screen

fades to a picture

of an accessible parking space.

Her voice drifts over

the image:

"Today, I went to a bookstore

in Hudson. As you know,

I use my transport chair

when I'm on my own

because it's easier

for me to lift.

I parked in a spot

with my accessible parking permit,

got out, and pulled

the chair from the trunk.

But then this person

said, *What are you doing?*

She screamed in my face.

She told me I was faking.

She said I didn't *really*

need a wheelchair.

In her eyes,

I wasn't disabled.

Here's the thing:

People think they know

our bodies like their own.

But they don't.

Only we understand

our bodies.

We know what they need,

even though lots of other people—

strangers and doctors and teachers—

think it's their job to know

our bodies. Like it's a language

they can just study

and know. They can't.

So to all my spoonies

out there, remember:

you know your bodies.

You know your bodies.

You know your bodies."

Looking at the Facts

In science, I learn the difference
        between facts
        and theories.

A fact is something that is
        absolutely, 100 percent true
        —you can prove it.

For example,
        the Earth orbits around the sun
        and this means a year has passed.

We have proof of this.
        We celebrate it.
        We know it as fact.

A theory sometimes uses facts
        to make a guess
        about something.

An example of facts as evidence:

        Riley's parents decide to sue
        the school district. (Fact.)

        Mr. Wilson gets called to
        a meeting about the lawsuit. (Fact.)

        Riley observes Mr. Wilson's face
        redden like an angry tomato. (Fact.)

Riley's Theory

Riley texts me
at two in the morning.
We've got trouble.

She tells me about
how the venue for prom
was changed to this
ballroom downtown.
The dance floor
is in the basement.

There isn't an elevator.
Stairs to get in,
more to get out.

No wheelchair access.
No way our bodies
could make it work.

My stomach twists
as I take in the facts:
we can't go to prom.

Riley's theory states that:

>Mr. Wilson was so mad
>he asked the school board
>to host the prom
>in the ballroom building–
>
>It would be
>cheaper.
>
>But he didn't tell them
>that it wasn't
>accessible
>for people like us.

Therefore, In Conclusion

Riley wants to fight back.

Protest.
Tell the news.

Make
a
fuss.

But My Theory?

If we make
Mr. Wilson
angrier,

he'll take
away anything
good

we have left.

Roll Over

"I made these last night,"
Riley says, handing me
a flyer in the hall
the next morning.

In big, red letters,
it says,

DON'T LET
MR. WILSON
ROLL OVER
OUR RIGHTS.

Below the words
is a graphic
of stairs with an X
through them.

There's information
about a protest
outside of school
in one week.

"Do you think
people will come?"
Riley asks.

I feel like I have
a tacky
wad of gum
stuck in my throat.

"Maybe we should just talk
to Mr. Wilson," I say.

"I'm sure he didn't realize
about the ballroom."

Riley's mouth tightens.

"He knew exactly
what he was doing,"
she says.

"Maybe we should stay
home from prom.
Order pizza, watch some
superspoonie," I say.

"I don't understand
how you're not angry."

I think she's shaking her head.
But then I see that her entire body
is vibrating.

Riley is mad.
Really,
really
mad.

"This goes against
every single right
we have as
disabled people,"
she says.

　　"I guess," I say,
　　my voice small.

"You guess?"
Riley's voice rises,
c r a c k i n g
at the top.

Other students
are starting to stare.
The way they did
when I first started
using my chair.

　　"Maybe you should just
　　do the stupid essays.
　　Then we wouldn't be in
　　this mess at all,"
　　I say,
　　my cheeks burning.

"You know,"
Riley says, gripping
the push guard
of her wheel

hard enough
that her knuckles
lose color.

"Sometimes you sound

       just

            like

                  them."

    "Like who?"
    I ask.

    But I wish
    I didn't. I wish
    I could take
    back every
    word I've ever
    said. Swallow
    them up like
    an arcade
    machine
    taking tokens.

"Like Mr. Wilson.

Like the person
in superspoonie's video.

Like you're not
disabled."

Collision

In space, sound travels differently.

Sometimes, objects collide

    and the boom echoes

        in different speeds.

But I'm pretty sure
the entire solar system
could hear this collision.

All the beings,

all the planets,

all the stars in the sky:

listening to the final echo
of two friends smashing together
and breaking apart.

Phenomenon

Dad read a lot of science books to me

when I was smaller.

I learned about this word–

phenomenon,

which is something

like an event, or fact, or thing

that we can see happening

before our eyes,

even if we don't understand it

just quite yet.

There's some phenomenon

happening in the universe

and I don't understand it.

Dad's stopped returning my calls.

We're further away than ever.

Superspoonie hasn't posted any videos

and everyone's getting worried.

I tell Mom that I won't use my wheelchair

for prom, and she doesn't want me to go.

Riley is getting ready to move.

We're not speaking anymore.

Gravity feels a bit heavier lately.

And I don't know how to resist

falling under its pull.

An Unexpected Meeting

Wednesday, I get a yellow slip of paper
　　　　from Ms. Johnson.

It has a room number and a time
　　　　next to my name.

"What's this?" I ask.
　　　　But she shrugs.

Says it's Official School Business
　　　　and to be there on time.

My body aches in time with my worries:
　　　　Did I do something wrong?

Am I failing a class?
　　　　Is it Mom? Mrs. C?

At the end of math, I wheel myself
　　　　slowly to the room.

I can't quite reach the handle
　　　　so I knock.

The door opens inward and a tall shadow
　　　　darkens the hallway's light.

I tilt my head up, past the creak in my neck,
　　　　to see Mr. Wilson, smiling down.

"You...wanted to meet?" I say.
　　　　My voice is barely a whisper.

"Come on in, Ms. Brennan," Mr. Wilson says.
        He moves to sit behind his desk
        in a large, gray swivel chair.

I can't make it all the way in his office.
        The doorway is too small
        for my wheelchair frame.

So we have to meet like this, then:
        Him– nestled and comfortable.
        Me–half inside, half outside.

"You might have heard that Riley MacDonald
        is leaving the district after a...
        disagreement with the school."

I wonder if he can hear my heart pulsing
        through my rib cage.

"I understand you were friends?" he asks.
        He wears a sour smile.
        "We were," I say.

"Ah," he says. The smile grows.
        "There was some talk
        of protest from students.

Rumors, I thought.
        But I found this."
        He holds up one of Riley's flyers.

"Do you know anything about this?"
           he asks. He tilts his head.

The room feels tight. The weight of the door
           presses on my wheels.

I have to activate the brakes so I don't roll
           right out of the room.

"I'm not sure," I say. I avoid his eyes.
           I am hot with shame.

Shame

for being part of this,
for making a scene,
for bringing attention
to my not-normal body.

Shame

for not speaking up
for Riley
and all the other disabled
students.
For myself.

Shame

for all I am
and all
I am not.

Smart Girl

"Now, you're a smart girl, Ms. Brennan,"
        Mr. Wilson says.

"You understand that a protest over a silly dance
        would reflect poorly on the school.

And it is a disruption to the other students
        who are trying to learn."

I feel my stomach meet my throat—my body,
        closing on itself like an accordion.

"I want you to do well here, Natalie. I wouldn't
        want you in a bad situation.

A situation that could have serious consequences."
        "Like the protest," I say.

"Yes. Exactly that," he says. "I will say this:
        if you can ensure this protest
        doesn't happen,

I'll see what I can do about getting
        you that laptop for assignments."

Give In

My hand spasms
in response to the idea
that I wouldn't have pain
taking notes
if only I were allowed
to type.

At home, I use
Mom's work laptop,
even though she's
not supposed to let
anyone else use it.

But if I had my own laptop...

She wouldn't have to
worry about getting
in trouble.

It's too good to be true.

I think about my options,
and I realize that
Mr. Wilson isn't really
giving me any.

I have to take down the flyers.

Sometimes,

it's easier
to give in
than to deal
with pain.

"Okay," I tell him.
"There won't be a protest."

"Excellent," he says.

I remember what Riley said—

        that I sound just like them.

        That I'm not on her side.

        Not even on my own side.

"Excellent," I say.

Secret Keeper

I started keeping secrets
when I got sick:

> what I felt
> what I thought
> what I could not do.

I thought I changed since then.

But it's so easy to slip
back into lies:

> I tell Mom I have to stay
> after school to clean
> my locker.

> I tell Mom I will get a ride
> from Riley's mom later.

> I tell Mom a lie so she doesn't
> have to know my pain.

Hiding

I hide in the bathroom
until everyone in the building
leaves for the day.

Then, I park my chair
and walk up and down
the hallways,
looking for protest flyers

       pinned on bulletin boards,

       stuck in locker jams,

       shoved under doors.

There are dozens of them—
       hundreds.

My nerves send zaps
up and down
my spine,
down my arms,
through my legs.

I shove the pain to the side.

It's not important right now.

This body
isn't
important.

Wish

I wish I could tuck myself away
with the recycled papers.
Be reprocessed.
Be reborn.

I forget what I felt like
in my prom dress.

I want to be invisible again.

I don't want to stand out anymore.

>   I could be on Mr. Wilson's
>   good side.

>   I could be friends with
>   Madison and Abby again.

>   I could go to prom.
>   Ditch the wheelchair
>   in an empty bathroom.

My body,
hidden.

Its secrets,
unknown.

I guess the worst secrets
are the ones I keep from myself.

Dead Batteries

I leave the protest papers
at the bottom of a bin in school
and start the ride home.

It's about two miles
and my wheelchair goes
about as fast as a skateboard.

I'll be back before Mom
or Mrs. C will know
that something is not right.

But as I reach the city fountain,
two blocks from Riley's house
and the halfway point

between home and school,
the chair starts to slow.
The battery symbol is on red.

It always needs a charge
after a long day, just like me.
I keep pushing forward.

My breath comes in heavy huffs,
my sweaty palm slipping on the joystick.
"No, no, no," I say. "Come on."

Wheels: stop.
Battery: dead.
Wheelchair Girl: stranded.

Rocket Fuel

I think about how space shuttles
always have extra fuel,
just in case.

Their journeys
are long as they slingshot
out of the atmosphere.

I sit near the fountain for a long time—
long enough that the sky looks
watercolor with its pinks and purples.

Mom and Mrs. C will start to wonder
about me now. Mom might even call
Mrs. MacDonald.

But then every secret
would unravel,
and I can't let that happen.

I start to walk. One step. One more.
I wonder if someone will take
my chair again.

My legs shake
and my mind feels
crowded.

I start to make a checklist
of my bones,
the ones I've dislocated.

Then I count how many bones
shift as I continue forward.
I look behind me after a while.

I can still see the fountain,
like a pencil smudge in the distance.
I haven't gone too far, but it feels

as though I've traveled
an entire galaxy
on foot.

Obstacle

I start to see stars
behind my eyelids.

I catch myself before
I fall to the ground
completely.

The skin of my palm
blooms red
as it opens.

I lower myself onto the grass.

I think about Mom.
I whisper, "I'm sorry,"
into the air.

I think about Mrs. C,
how she puts her body
through so much
just so I won't
have to.

I think about Mr. Wilson
and a laptop that I know
he won't ever let me have.

I think about Riley.

I remember something
from one of the times
we hung out at the mall.

The Question:

We were in the food court
of the mall,

bumping wheels,

    giddy.

I asked, "If you could fix your body,
       like, no pain, no limitations,
       would you?"

I knew my answer would be yes.

Riley's Answer:

"When I was younger, maybe I would say yes.
Having medical issues isn't fun.

I hated the stares the most. People
looking at me like my life was so sad.
That since I was disabled, I had to live

a miserable existence. But as I got older,
I learned that my body's not what's wrong
with our world.

You know what bothers me most now?
Yeah, the pain sucks, sure, but you know
what's worse?

Worrying about if I can go somewhere
with my friends. Will it have an elevator?
One that works?

Will the doorways be big enough?
Will there be accessible parking spaces?

Will we be able to stay and have fun?
Or will it be my fault that we have to go
because I can't get into the building?

Nobody wants to be the friend who
leaves the Wheelchair Girl out of plans

because she can't do stairs,
or the accessible train is down,
or the sidewalks are too bumpy.

It's taken a lot of work for me to know
that this isn't my fault. That if something
doesn't work out, it's not my body's fault.

It's inaccessibility. It's how everything
is built for people who can move.

If I could get into any building,
go anywhere without worry,
I would be limitless."

Riley had patted my shoulder.

"It's okay to not want to be disabled,"
she said. "But ask yourself why.

What's the real

obstacle

that's stopping you?"

What's the obstacle stopping me?
Right now: pain.

Why am I in pain?

Because I've pushed my body too far.

Why did I push my body?

Because I couldn't charge my wheelchair
at school. Ran out of battery

because Mr. Wilson
said that I could have the one thing
that would help with pain

      if I covered up the truth
      about what he was doing.

Because I pushed my body to its limits
again and again and again
to make the world

      more comfortable
      with how it treats me.

Is the obstacle that I'm disabled?

Or is it that everybody else
isn't quite sure how to make
a society that works
for disabled people, too?

Get Up

Riley's known this truth
for so long.

This is why
she wanted to protest.

I tell myself I have to
     get up.

But my head spins and my body
     is rooted
     to
     the
     ground.

I have to
     get up.

I could walk to Riley's, I think.

I could tell her everything.

I start to sit up, feel my joints
resist and complain, and–

"Natalie!" I hear.

Then, I feel gentle hands
assisting me, guiding me up
and into my wheelchair.

I look behind me and there's
Mrs. MacDonald and Mom.

And next to them,

the person who said my name,

is Riley.

Back in Orbit

The Prom Squad is back together–

> except this time,
> it's because of me.

And I'm in trouble.

The four of us–

> Mom,
> & Mrs. MacDonald
> & Riley
> & me–

sit in Riley's living room.

My wheelchair charges in the corner.

> I can feel my heart
> throb in every joint,
> every muscle I have.

I am the most seen

> I've ever been.

I tell them everything:

> my meeting with Mr. Wilson.

> My secret aches and pain.

> The way it feels to be sick
> and to know that my life
> has changed forever.

Mom hugs me after that,

> real tight, like she's finally
> not afraid to hurt me.

Mrs. MacDonald makes us tea,

> and I feel warm,
> soft, from her kindness.

Riley avoids my eyes,

> and I just wish
> she would say something.

Mom must sense the silence between us

      so she gets up
      to help Mrs. MacDonald
      in the kitchen.

I'm not sure what to say,

      or if there's anything to say,
      but the quiet in the room
      feels like we've been put
      in a space vacuum:

      no sound,
      no movement.

      I clear my throat.

      "Superspoonie hasn't posted
      since that last video you shared,"
      I say.

Riley looks up.

"The spoonies are getting worried,"
she says.

      "Yeah," I say.

      "I guess we never really run out
      of caring-spoons, do we?"

Riley smiles a little,

and I feel the world
tilt back into orbit.

"So," I say, pausing for a moment.

"Do you think the protest
has room for one more?"

This time, her face lights up,

and I know then that we're okay.
That she forgives me.

Ready to Fight

We are ready to fight

Mr. Wilson,

and the prom injustices,

and work toward disability rights

together.

That's when it hits me.

> "I just had an idea," I say.
>
> "But we're going to have to
>
> work fast.
>
> And we're going to need
>
> a lot of spoons."

The Protest Prom

Riley and I spend every minute
of the next week together.
We make posters
and send out emails.

We refresh superspoonie's
social media pages
in between bites
of cinnamon-sugar pretzels.

The protest has turned
into a disability-positive
prom. We send invitations
to all the schools in the area.

Mr. Wilson nearly explodes
when he sees Riley return
for the protest prom planning party.
She wiggles her fingers
at him in a wave.

We see the school superintendent
knock on his door one day.
When Mr. Wilson finally
comes out of his office,
he looks smaller, somehow.

Return of the Prom Squad

Prom Squad becomes
Protest-Prom Squad.

Riley's mom gets
the perfect place
for our big idea—

a big barn
with no stairs
and plenty of room
for wheelchairs.

Mrs. C contacts all her friends
and they promise
pastas
pastries
pizzas.

Mom makes playlists
of perfect dance music.

It's all coming together.

We've all come together.

The Best Part

"Check this out," Riley says
the morning of the protest prom.

She has her phone in her hand.

We sent out invitations
to the superspoonie group chat
online and explained

      why we were having this prom

      why it's so important to us

      why we have to take a stand.

"It says that over 50
superspoonie fans
are coming to our prom!"

"Wait, Riley, look," I say.

I point to one of the hundreds
of message notifications we've gotten.

"Look at the username," I say.
"HannahOnWheels. That's
superspoonie's girlfriend!"

"Read it!" she says.

Dear Riley and Natalie,

We love how hard you're working
to make prom accessible and to fight
for the rights we deserve as spoonies.

We wish we could be there,
but it's been all hospital visits
lately.

Hopefully you'll see
some new videos soon.

Until then, keep on
rolling forward.

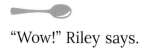

"Wow!" Riley says.

"Hospital visits?" I ask.

Riley knocks her head
lightly against mine.

"It's part of being sick.
Sometimes you feel
on top of the world.

And other times, it's a fight
to keep your body going."

I nod. I know exactly
what Riley means.

"You ready to fight?" she says.

I lift my head, look at her.
I bump my wheels
against hers.

Say, "Let's roll."

Out of This World

Mom, Mrs. C, and Mrs. MacDonald
take millions of pictures of:

the barn, decorated with the stars
I've had in my room forever.

The crowd of people—a total
of more than 200—

who use wheelchairs, canes,
joint splints, braces, prosthetics—

and the ones who don't use
anything at all.

Mostly, they take pictures
of me and Riley:

> serving punch,
> wheel-dancing,

> singing at the tip-top
> of our lungs,

> smiling so hard
> that I think

> you could see our

> bright, happy faces

> all the way from space.

Riley and I know
that she's leaving

for St. Jude's Academy in a month.
We know that this night

will end, and the last song
will play, and our legs

will ache with the memory
of dancing, even if we

aren't using them so much.
We know that this won't fix

everything that's wrong
with the school,

with Mr. Wilson,
with the prom that

is still happening
despite this.

But in this moment,
we feel out of this world,

finally able to be ourselves—
no limitations. No gravity

holding us down.

Spoonies, IRL

The night slows,
      the sky darkening.

Riley calls me over
      to a group of people

she's talking to near the
      cardboard cutout of the moon.

"Nat, this is Shawn,
         Deja,
         Kate,
         and
         William.

They all went to our school,"
      Riley says.

"Went?" I ask.

"Once upon a time," Deja says.
      She shifts on her feet and

I notice that she wears a
      prosthetic leg on the left.

"Tell her what you told me,"
      Riley says.

"All of us here," Kate starts, "had to leave
      because of Mr. Wilson's rules.

None of us wanted to write essays
        for gym credit."

"And whenever our parents would try
        to speak out on how unfair it was,

Mr. Wilson would make us think
        that it was our fault

because we didn't do
        the assignment," Deja says.

"This has been going on for too long,"
        Riley says.

Shawn and William nod.
        "But if all of us spoke up..."

"Something might finally change,"
        Kate says.

I realize that Riley is looking to me
        for approval.

I think about last time—
        how not saying anything

ended in more pain.
        "I'm in," I say.

Riley grins, says, "Excellent."
        I grin, say, "Excellent."

How Bright We Can Burn

The sun has barely
peeked over the roof
of the school
on Monday morning,
but we're ready.

Riley and I in front,
our galaxy of support
behind us—everyone
from our protest-prom
who lived in the area.

We work our way down
the hall.

Wet tires,
damp canes,
blazing a trail.

We gather outside
of Mr. Wilson's office.
His secretary
arrives first.

"Oh, my," she says.
She's not sure
where to look.
I think back
to when Riley took me in
the crystal shop at the mall.

We don't make the space
uncomfortable
with our disabled bodies.
But the space can make
our disabled bodies feel
uncomfortable.

"We'd like to schedule
a meeting with Mr. Wilson,"
I say. "The soonest possible."

"And can I ask what this
is about?" she says.

"We have a list
of the things that need
to change around here,"
Riley says.

"Well. Let me see
what I can do," she says.
Riley and I move to the door
and neither of us can
fit through.

I look at her. She holds up a finger
to the secretary.
"This," I say, gesturing
to the too-small doorframe,
"will be the first change
of many."

The galaxy behind us murmurs,
agreeing, vibrating with energy.

I smile at Riley.
She takes my hand.

I look behind us,
to the different bodies
we all own: whole,
complete, beautiful.

We're all bursting
with heat.

On fire.

Ready to fall from the sky,
as though we are stars
come to show everyone

how bright

we can burn.

WANT TO KEEP READING?

If you liked this book, check out another book
from West 44 Books:

Tough as Lace
By Lexi Bruce

ISBN: 9781978595514

Who I Am

My name is Lacey,
but I am not
like lace.

I am bruises.
I am turf burn.
I am mud-caked cleats
and I am sweat stains.

I am lightning
on the lacrosse field.
Swerving
around defenders
and shooting
the ball past goalies.

I am not
delicate and for show.
I am not so special
that mud will ruin me.

I am not here
to look pretty
at the dining room table.

I am here to do
what I have to.

I am here to win.

Winning Together

After Friday afternoon practice,
I walk with my best friend–
and goalie–Jenna.
Head over to our favorite
hangout spot,
Rosie's Juice and Smoothie Bar.
Meet up with
my boyfriend,
Owen.

I notice him as soon
as we walk in.
He looks up
and waves at us.
Then runs
his fingers
through his messy,
dark hair.

He's sitting at a table,
sipping a mango-berry smoothie.
Reading *The Glass Menagerie*
for English on Monday.

He already ordered
my favorite smoothie for me,
mixed berry
with lots of ginger.

He closes his book
and kisses me
when I sit down
next to him.

Jenna goes up to the counter
to place her order.

"How was practice?"
Owen asks
as I take my first
sip of the smoothie.

"Really great,"
I say.
"I think
this is gonna be
my season!"

"I can't believe
I'm dating the greatest
lacrosse star
in the state,"
Owen says.

"Oh, cut it out.
You know that's
not true. I'm really only
the *second*-greatest
lacrosse star
in New York,"
I joke and kiss him.

We always tease
over which one of us
is a better player.

"Nope, you're definitely
the very best.
You're number one,
I swear.
Lacrosse my heart
and hope to die."

He winks.

I'd never tell him,
but his bad puns
are one of
my favorite
things
in the world.

I roll my eyes
and smile at him.
I love that he means it
when he tells me
I'm the best.